Mama's Saris

by **Pooja Makhijani** Illustrated by **Elena Gomez**

LITTLE, BROWN AND COMPANY

New York Boston

For my mother

P.M.

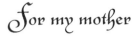

For Rukhsana Hanif and Aliyah Rafique

E.G.

Text copyright © 2007 by Pooja Makhijani
Illustrations copyright © 2007 by Elena Gomez

Little, Brown and Company

Hachette Book Group USA
1271 Avenue of the Americas, New York, NY 10020
Visit our Web site at www.lb-kids.com

First Edition: May 2007

Library of Congress Cataloging-in-Publication Data
Makhijani, Pooja.
  Mama's saris/ by Pooja Makhijani; illustrated by Elena Gomez.— 1st ed.
    p. cm.
  Summary: An East Indian American daughter pleads with her mother to be allowed to
wear one of her mother's colorful saris in honor of her seventh birthday.
  ISBN 0-316-01105-3
  1. East Indian Americans—Juvenile fiction. [1. East Indian Americans—Fiction. 2. Mothers
and daughters—Fiction. 3. Saris—Fiction. 4. Clothing and dress—Fiction.] I. Gomez,
Elena, ill. II. Title.
PZ7.M282545Mam 2005
[E]—dc22   2005003827

10 9 8 7 6 5 4 3 2 1

Book design by Alison Impey

TWP

Printed in Singapore

The illustrations for this book were done in acrylics.
The text was set in Sanvito MM, and the display type is Civilite MJ.

Author's Note

When I was a child, my friends and I used to pull out our mothers' fancy clothes and play "dress up." I remember all of us trying on hats and shawls and scarves and gloves, falling over in leather pumps and getting tangled in colorful costume jewelry, and putting on red lipstick (that always landed on our chins) and pink blush (that frequently found its way to our noses).

For me, it was my mother's saris—her dress-up clothes—that were captivating. They were every color you can imagine—apricot, olive green, sepia—and had names like Baluchari (saris woven with animals and kings and scenes from Indian myths), Banarasi (timeless silks from the northern city of Varanasi), Kalamkari (hand-painted saris), Kantha (quilted saris), and Zardosi (saris embroidered with real gold). She wore them only for special occasions, unlike her mother or mother-in-law, for whom the sari was an everyday garment. So on birthdays, Diwali (Hindu New Year), family weddings, and trips to the temple, my mother would take out the bag, her bindis, and her bangles, and wrap herself in yards of material. Since her saris were too much for me to handle, I would instead steal her dupattas, decorative scarves that she mixed and matched with various outfits, and drape them the way I thought a sari would be arranged. This compromise sufficed until I was tall enough to wear her saris and, finally, old enough to buy my own.

I wrote *Mama's Saris* after realizing that my own fascination with my mother's fancy clothes was not unique. It seemed as if each of my female friends, regardless of ethnicity or age, remembers being captivated by her mother's grown-up clothes. By dressing up like their mothers (and emulating everything else that they did), they would be just as beautiful, too.

Glossary of Hindi Words in *Mama's Saris*

Note: *th* should be pronounced as the sound in "this" or "the."

bindi (bin-*THEE*) The decorative mark worn on the forehead of a Hindu woman. Traditionally, it was a red dot that served as a symbol of marriage; today it is considered a fashion accessory and is no longer restricted in color or shape.

chaniya choli (CHUN-EE-yaa cho-LEE) A flared skirt (chaniya) and tight-fitting blouse (choli), traditionally worn by women in the western Indian states of Gujarat and Rajasthan.

didi (*THEE*-thee) A term of respect for an elder sister, a female cousin, or female friend.

Diwali (*thi*-VAA-lee) Diwali signifies many different things to people across India, but everywhere it signifies the renewal of life. It is common to wear new clothes on the day of the festival. Diwali means "rows of lighted lamps," and the celebration is often referred to as the Festival of Lights. During this time, families light small oil lamps and place them around their homes in order to welcome the new year.

Masi (MAA-see) mother's sister.

Nanima (NAA-nee-maa) mother's mother.

sari (SAA-ree) The traditional dress of Indian women. It is a rectangular piece of cloth five to nine yards in length. The style, color, and texture of this cloth vary and it can be draped in many ways, depending on the woman's status, age, occupation, and religion, as well as the region where the woman lives.

"Mama, when can I wear a sari?" I jump onto my mother's bed and sit down. I watch her reach under the bed and pull out a leather suitcase. Inside are her saris — the yellow satin one she wore for Uma Didi's baby shower, the peach-colored one that is as fine as a spider's web, and my favorite, her red wedding sari, which I have only seen once because it is carefully wrapped in an old bedsheet.

"When you get older," she says, unzipping the suitcase and putting it on the bed.

"But I'm seven today! And we're having a party," I say. "That's why you're wearing one."

Mama only takes out her suitcase on special occasions. Nanima wears a sari every day, even when she sleeps. The folds and nooks of Nanima's saris hold lots of secrets. I always find coins tied into the ends and safety pins fastened on the inside, and I smell the scent of cardamom and sandalwood soap all over.

Mama flips open the top of the suitcase. I open my eyes wider and try to soak up all the colors.

"Will you help me choose one to wear?" she asks.

"Yes!" I say. Maybe after we have decided on hers, I can pick out one for me.

"How about this one?" She holds a purple sari up to her cheek.

"Mama, you'll look like an eggplant!" I laugh.

"This one?" Mama unfolds a black chiffon sari that shimmers like the nighttime sky.

"No, you wore that for Devi Masi's anniversary party."

"I can't believe you remember that!"

I always remember the saris my mother wears. For Diwali, she was wrapped in a lavender sari. The first time Nanima came to visit, she wore a magenta one with a herd of galloping deer embroidered on it.

I think Mama looks so pretty when she wears her saris. They are so different from the gray sweaters and brown pants that she wears to work every day.

"What about this one?" I point to a sari that I don't think I've seen before. It is orange like fire with edges that look like they have been dipped in red paint.

"I wore that sari the day we brought you home from the hospital." Mama smiles. "All your aunties and uncles came to greet you."

"Wear it again today!"

Mama unfurls it. It shines like the afternoon sun. I watch her tuck one end into her petticoat and pull the other end over her left shoulder. Then she folds the pleats, weaving the fabric into an accordion between her slim fingers.

I look down at my Mary Janes and corduroy jumper. I feel so plain next to her.

"Why can't I wear a sari?" I ask.

"You know saris are for grown-ups," she says. "Even if I fold the sari several times, it will spill off your shoulders and get tangled around your ankles. How will you walk or play on your new swing set?"

"But you never let me do anything," I say. "Yesterday you said I couldn't wear silver party shoes to school, even though you wear high heels to work every day."

"Why don't you wear your chaniya choli?" Mama suggests, holding the tight blouse and flowing skirt that hang in her closet. "You told me all the mirrors on the skirt make you feel like a princess."

"No! I am old enough to wear a sari, just like you," I say. "I don't need a night-light anymore, and I can pour my own glass of milk in the morning without spilling anything!"

Mama is silent for a long time. Then she says, "I remember the first time I wore one of Nanima's saris. It made me feel like a big girl."

"Please, Mama? Let me pick out a sari," I whisper. "I know which one I want to wear."

"Well, you are getting taller, and we could use lots of safety pins to secure all the tucks and pleats." Mama puts her arms around me. "Yes, you can wear a sari. But just today, because it's your birthday."

"Can I wear one again on my eighth birthday?"
I say. "By then I'll be as tall as you!"

Mama laughs. She sits beside her suitcase and
begins to show me the saris, one by one. Soon,
there is only one at the bottom of the bag.

"That's it!" I say. It's blue with gold flowers that
dance along the border.

"Stand up on the bed," she tells me. She wraps the fabric around me again and again. I try to look at myself in the mirror.

"Wait, you're not ready yet!" she says, grabbing my hands and squeezing them tightly. She pulls out a heart-shaped tin from her closet. Inside are her fancy bangles.

Mama slides six gold bangles onto my left arm. They are so big. When I put my arm down, they fall, jingling as they hit the floor.

"We'll have to ask Nanima to send new bangles to match this sari," Mama teases.

"Can I look in the mirror now?" I ask.

"Just one more thing," she says.

Mama opens the top drawer of her dresser and takes out a small box. Inside, stuck to little squares of plastic, are bindis in many different colors and shapes — circles, diamonds, and teardrops. She removes a glittery one and sticks it right between my eyebrows.

"Now you can look," she says, beaming.

I lean over to the mirror, gathering the sari carefully.

"So, what do you think?" she asks.

I feel like I am floating in an ocean of blue. The shiny material makes me sparkle. I think it looks beautiful. I run my fingers along the edge of my sari and turn to look into Mama's big brown eyes.

"I think I look like you!"